OCT   2000

MOUSE IN LOVE

by Robert Kraus

illustrated by
Jose Aruego and
Ariane Dewey

Orchard Books • New York

Orchard Books, A Grolier Company, 95 Madison Avenue, New York, NY 10016

Manufactured in the United States of America. Printed and bound by Phoenix Color Corp.
Book design by Mina Greenstein. The text of this book is set in 24 point Futura Medium.
The illustrations are ink, watercolor, and pastels.
10 9 8 7 6 5 4 3 2 1

Library of Congress Cataloging-in-Publication Data
Kraus, Robert, date.
Mouse in love / by Robert Kraus ; illustrated by Jose Aruego and Ariane Dewey.   p.   cm.
Summary: Mouse searches high and low for his true love, only to find her right next door.
ISBN 0-531-30297-0 (trade : alk. paper)—ISBN 0-531-33297-7 (lib. bdg. : alk. paper)
[1. Mice—Fiction. 2. Neighbors—Fiction. 3. Stories in rhyme.] I. Aruego, Jose, ill.
II. Dewey, Ariane, ill. III. Title.
PZ8.3.K864 Mo 2000 [E]—dc21 99-58611

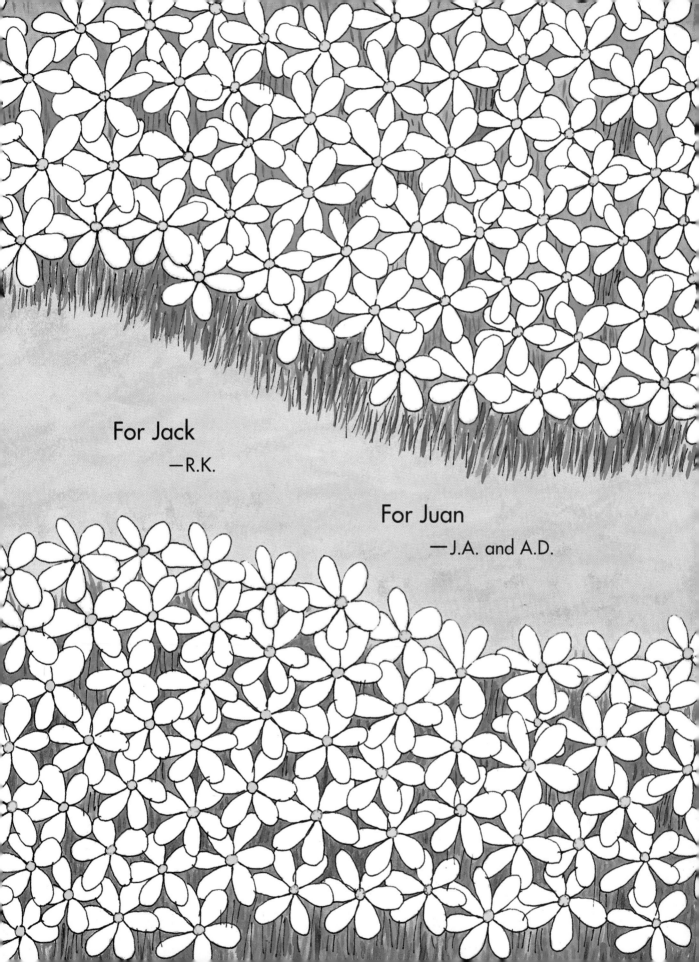

For Jack
—R.K.

For Juan
—J.A. and A.D.

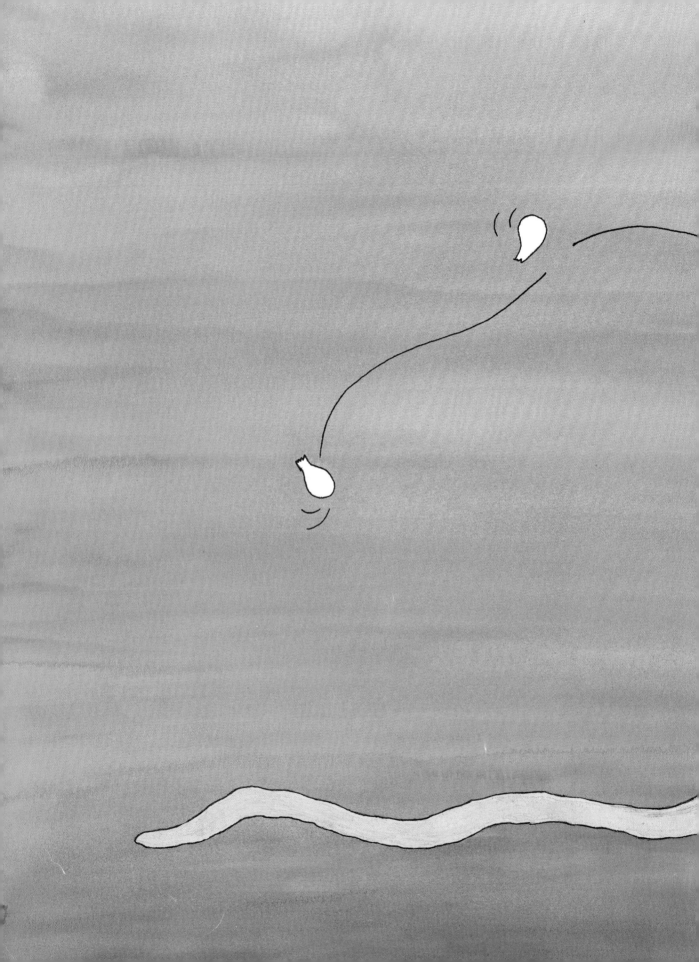

She loves me.
She loves me not.
She loves me.

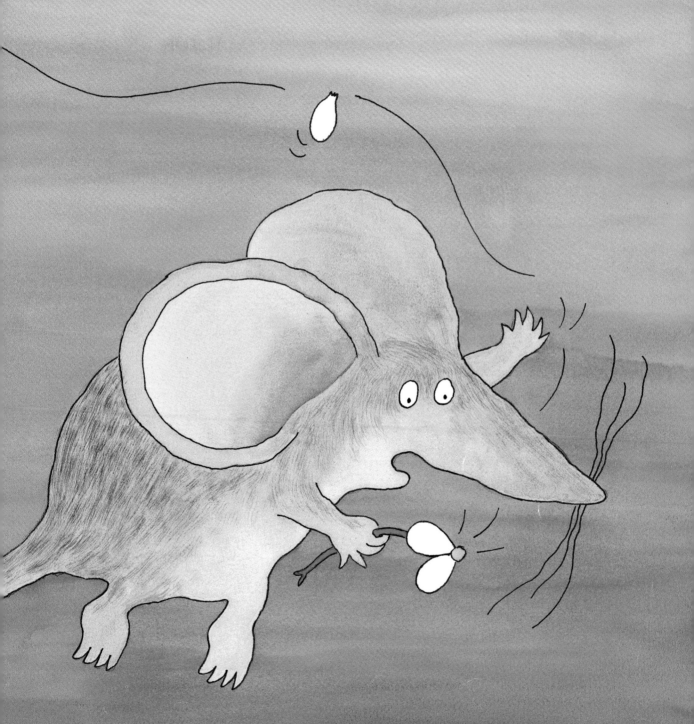

She loves me not.

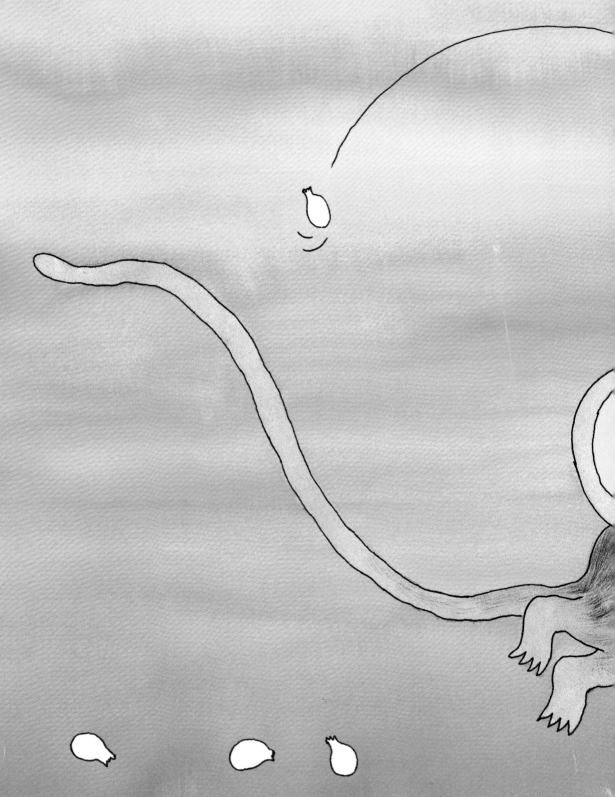

She loves me!

"Why so dreamy, little mouse?"

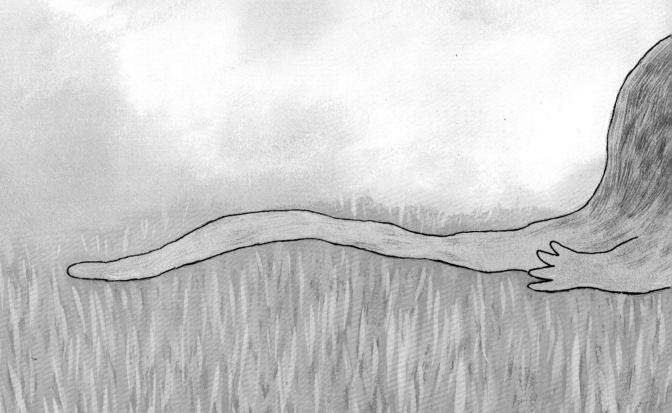

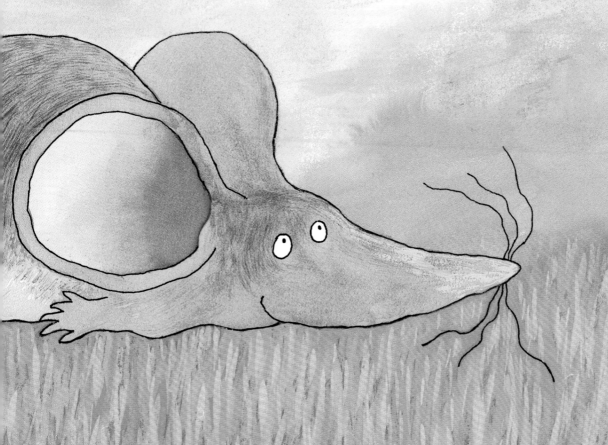

"I'm in love!"

"Who's the mouse?"

"She's the mouse of my dreams.
I've never met her.
But try as I may, I can't forget her."

"So what will you do?"

"Look for that mouse
and try to get her."

"Where will you find her?"

"Maybe she waits in a palace fine."

"Maybe she waits at the end of the line."

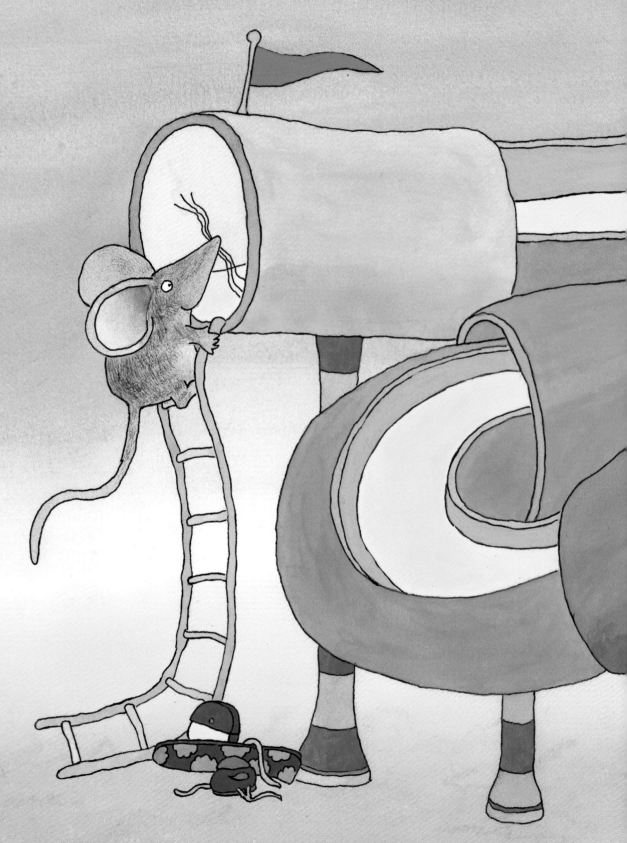

"How will you find her?"

"I'll travel by train."

"I'll travel by plane."

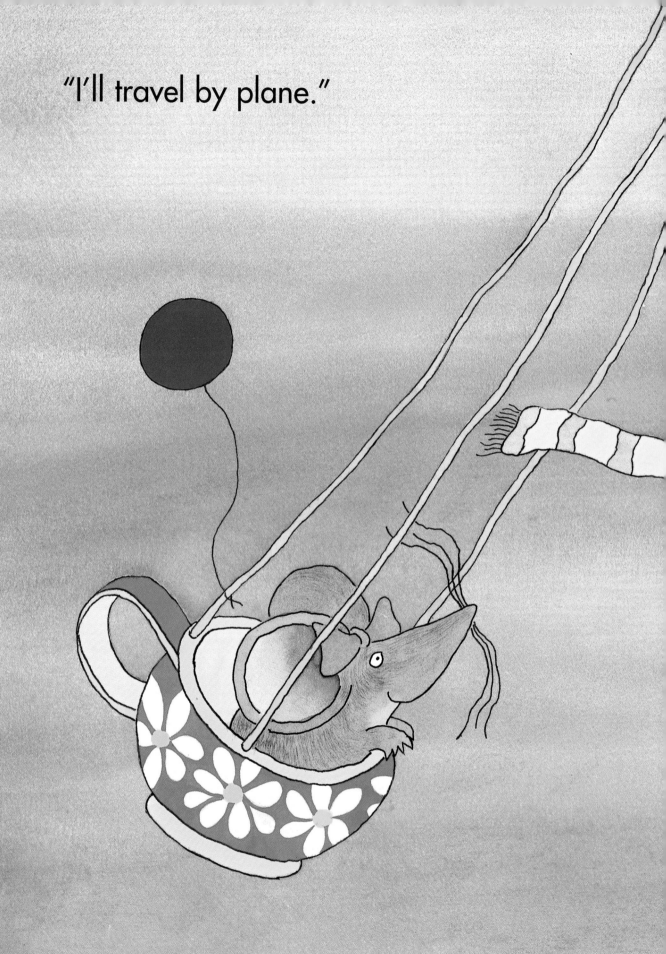

"I'll search on land,
sea, and air
until . . .

I find my mousie fair."

"Aren't you tired?"

"I'm pooped!"

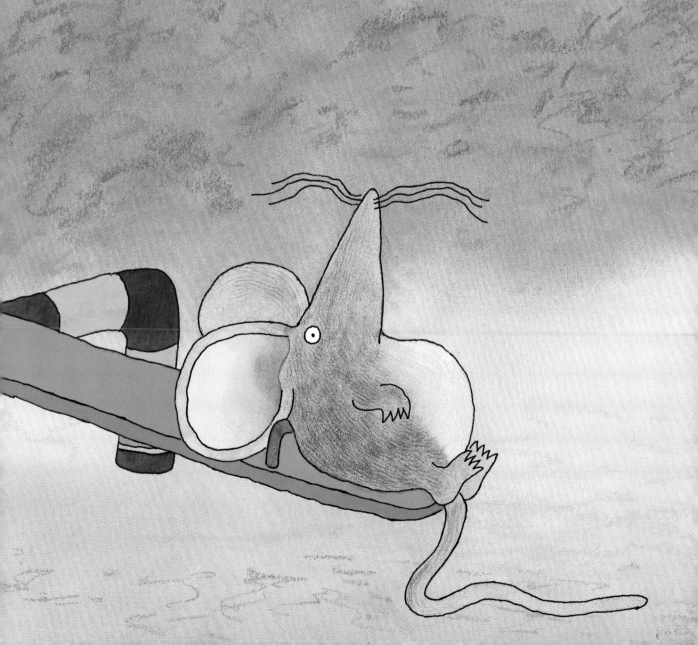

"Isn't it time for supper?"

"Oh, my gosh, I better hurry home!"

"I'm home at last and my feet are sore.

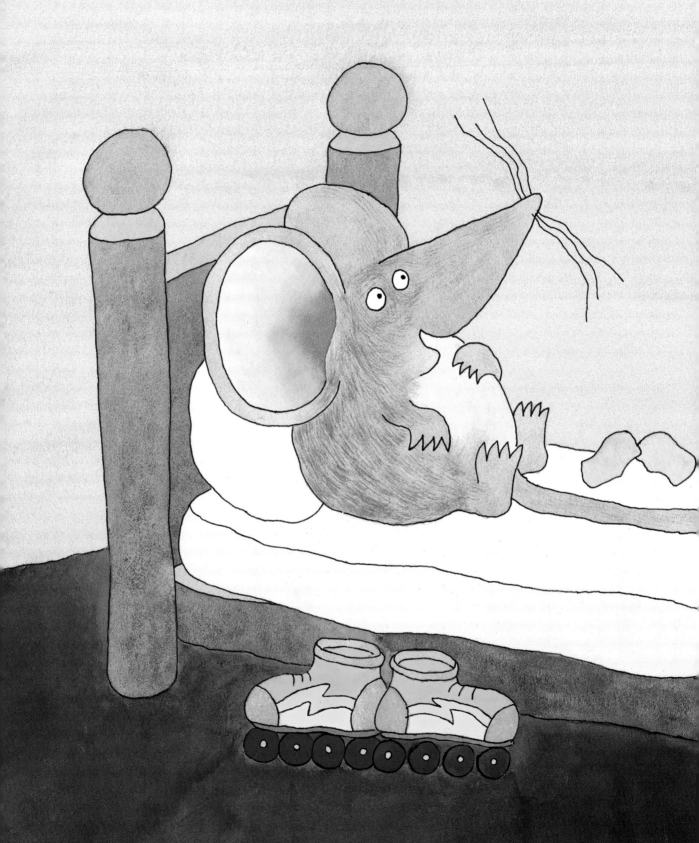

And guess what I've found?"

"What have you found?"

"The mouse I love . . ."

"is the mouse next door!"